# DUEL

## A MYSTERY BY
## DAVID GROSSMAN

### TRANSLATED BY BETSY ROSENBERG

Published by Bloomsbury, New York and London
Distributed to the trade by Holtzbrinck Publishers

Library of Congress Cataloging-in-Publication Data
Grossman, David.
Duel / by David Grossman ; translated by Betsy Rosenberg.
p. cm.
ISBN 1-58234-930-4 (alk. paper)
I. Rosenberg, Betsy, trans. II. Title.
PZ40.G76 D813 2004
892.4'36--dc22
2003047198

First U.S. Edition 2004
Printed in the U.S.A.

1 3 5 7 9 10 8 6 4 2

Bloomsbury USA Children's Books
175 Fifth Avenue
New York, New York 10010

All papers used by Bloomsbury Publishing are natural,
recyclable products made from wood grown in well-managed
forests. The manufacturing processes conform
to the environmental regulations of the country of origin.

## CHAPTER ONE

# Under the Bed

There were three of us: Jonny, the strongest boy in class, Sam, who was as daring as a Japanese pilot and knew how to wiggle his ears, and me. No wait. That's no good.

There were seven of us, seven adventurous, sharp-eyed sleuths. And we had a dog too, a big dog, really smart, who could shoot a gun if necessary and lie without blushing. Yes, together we were invincible, we were . . .

No, there weren't seven of us and there weren't three of us, or a dog either, for that matter. It was just me, myself and I, otherwise I might have felt a little safer under the bed in the Beit Hakerem Home for the Aged waiting for the bully of Heidelberg to arrive. I only wish there had been someone with me, someone who knew what to do in a pinch, someone with plenty of sleuthing experience and preferably a gun, or maybe a magnifying glass to look for prints on the body . . .

Frankly I was a little worried the body would turn out to be my own – to which I am more than a little attached – but I tried not to dwell on such melancholy thoughts, and stared ahead at the light coming from the crack below the door.

From my vantage point under the bed I could see, besides the door, a colourful rug, an old grey suitcase with two cloth belts and Mr Rosenthal's sneakers.

But I think I'd better explain myself first. I mean, whoever heard of starting a story under the bed? It isn't respectable, and it can get a little dusty too.

I was twelve years old when what I'm about to tell you took place. Today, sixteen years later, I still recall the pounding of my heart as I heard the approaching footsteps of the bully of Heidelberg University. Above me on the bed sat Heinrich Rosenthal, a little man, seventy years old, with a big white mane of hair, but under the bed I was very much alone, and I remember thinking in those moments of suspense, maybe Mom's right, maybe I should go out and make friends my own age instead of always hanging around by myself or with weird old people like Mr Rosenthal. My parents used to get upset that I never went to parties at school or scout meetings and things like that. All I was upset about was that they were upset. I was fine. The kids at school had stopped pestering me to join their games – maybe they were sick of me, or maybe they just didn't care.

I kept telling them I was fine, but Dad would come into my room at night and sit on the edge of my bed in silence, staring at me. That was awful, even worse than my noisy fights with Mom, who used to scream at me that sometimes I acted more like an old man than a twelve-year-old boy. She didn't know Mr Rosenthal. That man was as spry as any twenty year old. His motto was: Life begins at seventy.

I met Mr Rosenthal at the beginning of the school year. Our home room teacher had divided us into groups of 'volunteers'. One of her suggested projects for us was to make friends with an elderly person.

As soon as Mom heard that out of all the school projects I had chosen 'to adopt' some old man and keep him company twice a week, she said, 'Wouldn't you know it?' which is short for: 'Wouldn't you know it? That boy can't leave his books and that darned rabbit of his for five minutes to go out and play soccer with someone his own age, oh no, not him, he has to make friends with a senior citizen, and what's more, he's doing it to spite me.' That's the unabridged version. 'Wouldn't you know it,' is a lot more to the point, you have to admit. But it didn't do her much good, because the next day I signed up with three other kids from my class to visit the Beit Hakerem Home for the Aged in Jerusalem.

Wait. There's something I want to say. I know some kids don't like to spend time with old people because old people are wrinkled and smelly and slow. What they don't seem to realise is that the reason old people look so neglected sometimes is that there's nobody around to take care of them and love them. It's like a simple rule of grammar, when someone deserts you, you start to feel deserted. That's what I kept hearing from the old people at the Home while I waited for Mr Rosenthal. Their friends and their colleagues, everyone deserted them once they moved into the Home. Even their own children stopped visiting after a time. They felt as if they'd been blotted out of everyone's heart. I have more to say on the subject, but it will have to wait.

Because just then, I heard the sound of heavy footsteps outside Mr Rosenthal's door. From where I was I could see Mr Rosenthal's spindly ankles trembling in his sneakers. I knew he was as frightened as I was, even though he'd told me at least seven times that it was uncontrollable rage that was making him tremble. He'd also told me at least fourteen times that the bully of Heidelberg wore size 17 shoes, that he'd been an expert marksman in his student days in Germany, and could lift all twelve volumes of the medical encyclopaedia with one hand; he also told me about the time Schwartz punched five German students in the teeth for making anti-Semitic remarks.

And he told me a couple of other horrific stories that day, his face burning red under his ruffled white hair. Then he pounded his fist in his palm, seething in a heavy German accent, 'Let him dare walk in here! I'll teach him to threaten me! A thief he calls me – me, a thief! The brute! The beast! I'll beat the "chutzpah" out of him!' This was a bit strange coming from someone like Heinrich Rosenthal who was about as muscular as a schoolboy. I mean, even though he was in pretty good shape for his age and used to swim laps every day in the heated pool at the Hebrew University, and even though he used to tease me that my favourite sport was blinking every time I turned the page, my feeling was that if it came to a match between my 'old guy' and the free-style-encyclopaedia-lifting-bully, Rosenthal didn't stand a chance. When I gently hinted as much, he sneered at me and said that if I was such a coward I could either go home or wait for him outside till after the terrible battle, and then help him roll the remains of Rudy Schwartz down the corridor. But I could tell from the bitterness in his voice how frightened he must be, which is why I informed him straight out that I would stay, no matter what.

Wordlessly he walked over to me and shook my hand. I saw his lips compress, a sign that he was touched. Then came a silence when courage, friendship and determination were welded together in our handshake. But as soon as we let go I felt paralysed with fear again, and I saw Mr Rosenthal's shoulders droop a little too. He said that it was wrong of him to have involved me in this mess, that there was no way of knowing how it would turn out, not where a brute like Rudy Schwartz was concerned, and that maybe I really ought to go home. I told him that was out of the question, I was staying. I wasn't going to leave him alone with that total bully from Heidelberg, not after everything I'd heard about him and the strange threatening letter he'd written to Mr Rosenthal. I mean, I wasn't so tough or anything, but this way at least we would be two against one, which doubled the chances of one of us coming out of this alive to tell the story of the battle to future generations – or past generations – like my mom and dad.

And that was how we arrived at the same devious idea: I would hide under the bed till we discovered what Rudy Schwartz's intentions were, and then I would jump out and triumph over evil, or at least kick it in the shins.

Actually we already knew what his

intentions were because he'd spelled them out pretty clearly in the letter Mr Rosenthal received that morning.

The letter, now lying on the table, said, 'You are a miserable thief! Unless you return her mouth to me by seven o'clock this evening, I will take it away from you by force, and nothing will stop me.' And in the margin there were three words written in red ink that had a very peculiar ring, 'Honour or Death', and below, the signature – Rudy Schwartz.

## CHAPTER TWO

# Still Under the Bed

When a person changes his view of the world, unusual notions are apt to enter his mind. Take me for instance. Lying on my belly under Mr Rosenthal's bed in the Beit Hakerem Home for the Aged, I reflected that the world looks pretty scary from this level, the level of the floor. The wastebasket seemed to be as big as a barrel; the old grey suitcase loomed before me, huge as a closet; only the feet of Mr Rosenthal dangling down from the bed were as small as usual. Then it occurred to me that maybe the reason children are afraid sometimes is that everything looks so enormous to them. And maybe the reason old people often feel intimidated is because the world is so modern, so fast-moving. Even Mr Rosenthal, spry and up-to-date though he is, says he's afraid of elevators because they didn't have them in his day. I think he might be kidding though. He certainly doesn't seem to have trouble with other modern devices.

I might have gone on reflecting like this for a long time. Mom says that some people sink in thought, I drown in it, which may be true to a certain extent, only just then I had good reason to worry: it was one minute to seven, and the footsteps had come to a halt behind the door; Mr Rosenthal and I, above and below the bed respectively, knew that Rudy Schwartz, the bully of Heidelberg University, was standing outside, fuming mad. And when an expert marksman who wears a size 17 shoe stands fuming mad behind your door, you have at least two real causes for worry.

But it was still one whole minute to seven. I knew this, because I set my watch by the radio, which was set according to Mr Rosenthal's watch – or so at least Mr Toussia, the director of the Beit Hakerem

Home used to say. Mr Rosenthal and his watch were so accurate that Mr Toussia would only ring the dinner bell in the dining room when he saw Mr Rosenthal coming down the stairs. And since there was one whole minute left, and Rudy Schwartz was German like Mr Rosenthal, I knew that he would wait in the hallway till seven o'clock on the nose. Seven o'clock, he'd written in the letter that now lay on the table, so even though he'd called Mr Rosenthal 'A miserable thief,' and printed 'honour or death' in blood red ink at the bottom, Rudy Schwartz would never dream of knocking on the door before the appointed time.

Fear can make each minute seem like an eternity (or at least five minutes), which is why I think I'll break off here to explain who Rudy Schwartz the bully is and what he wants from Mr Rosenthal.

As I already told you, I met Mr Rosenthal through our school campaign to 'adopt the elderly' when I signed up as a volunteer together with a few of my classmates.

The biggest problem for elderly people in a place like the Home is the boredom and the loneliness, which is why it's so important to have someone look in on them. There were four of us from my class when we started off at the beginning of the year, but three months later I was the only one left. The others said they didn't have the time to spend with their adopted old people, who weren't that nice in any case; but I knew it was just hard for them to sit there for a whole hour listening to a lot of boring stories. At our age things seem to happen so fast that we're afraid we're going to miss something if we're not on the ball every second, which makes it kind of hard to 'switch over' to a much slower rhythm, the rhythm of old age.

Don't think I'm blaming the kids who dropped out of the project. I know it would have been just as hard for me in their position. Mom kept saying I'd done more than enough as far as she was concerned, and that it was high time I made friends with someone whose age was not a multiple of 35. Not that she had anything against the multiplication table – or against volunteering either, for that matter; but she did think I was forgetting to attend to myself with all my charitable activities, and she couldn't for the life of her understand why I had to get so involved with elderly people, or why I made so few friends of my own age. At this point Dad would join in and tell me about how long it took him to make friends when he immigrated to Israel as a twelve-year-old boy who didn't know Hebrew. Dad talks a lot about that period in his life, and I think that even now at the age of forty he aches with the humiliating memory of the child he was.

I tried to explain that I wasn't unhappy, that I liked my life the way it was. Besides, I hadn't always been this unsociable, as they knew very well. What about my best friend Elisha who'd moved to Haifa, leaving me with an irrational feeling of anger? Couldn't they get it through their heads that there are times when I just need to be alone, when there's a lot I have to figure out about myself and about the world?

But the reason I didn't mind going to see Mr Rosenthal once or twice a week was that I simply enjoyed it; he never let me feel that I was there to help him – it was usually the other way around, he made life more fun for me. I didn't talk about this with my parents. It's hard for me to express some-thing that complicated in words; I mean I can write it down, as I'm doing now, or as I did in my letters to Elisha, but I can't just stand up and say it out loud. Sometimes I'm afraid the words I say out loud will crumble in the air, and that's why I may have to leave out certain details of this story, though I think you'll understand me all the same.

But I'd better hurry.

Because just then there were three loud raps on the door, as though someone were knocking with a large, open palm. From down the corridor came the sound of the seven o'clock news beeps. The bully of Heidelberg University was right on time, as I knew he would be. Mr Rosenthal shuffled his feet. The bed above me creaked. His worn old sneakers steered toward the table, their prows pointing at the door. I figured he was standing beside the letter he'd received that morning, and I also guessed he was holding his shoulders high to make himself look as big and threatening as possible. I could hear the strain in his voice when he said, 'Enter, Mr Schwartz,' and then the door opened and there in the doorway stood the biggest pair of shoes I've ever seen in my life. They looked like two small ships sailing in my direction, into the room that is. There was such a deep silence I was afraid my heart would burst in my chest, or further down than that even, and suddenly the door slammed shut, and I heard a strange voice, a harsh, cracked voice say, 'Mr Rosenthal, I have come for Edith's mouth.' And Mr Rosenthal answered anxiously, 'I'm sorry Mr Schwartz, I have only her eyes, as you very well know.'

And had I not heard all about it from Mr Rosenthal an hour before, I would surely have thought they'd both gone stark raving mad.

## CHAPTER THREE

# Edith's Eyes

From my look-out under the bed (normally the habitat of dust balls and slippers) I could not see Rudy Schwartz's face, only his enormous shoes and the grey cuffs of his trousers.

I admit it isn't easy telling a detective story with such meagre details as these, but I'm afraid they're all I have. And I definitely agree with you that it's high time for the writer – me, as it happens – to crawl out from under the bed where he's been hiding for the past two chapters, and start proving himself. But this was not the best moment to jump out and reveal myself, and of course, I never dreamed I would someday want to describe the events taking place, let along divide them into chapters. Actually it wasn't so hard to follow what was going on from under the bed. I could see their feet, so I knew exactly where they were standing at all times (in case the police asked me to reconstruct the scene later on); besides, Mr Rosenthal's suitcase was right in front of me, and in it, I knew, lay the key to the entire mystery.

Let me explain something.

The first time I met Mr Rosenthal, I asked him to tell me the story of his life. I figured he'd want to talk about his memories. Elderly people usually do, which is normal, I guess, because once you stop doing things, all you have left is the memory of the things you used to do. But when I asked Mr Rosenthal, he put his hand on my shoulder and said: 'Friend David, what I've done with my life is done. Maybe some day when I'm old, I'll have the time to tell you about it. But the important question now is, what am I doing with my life today, right?'

That's what he said, as he squeezed my shoulder so hard I was forced to admit he was right. And then I started worrying: okay, if he wasn't going to talk about himself, how were we doing to spend our time together? My fears were groundless, though, and I quickly discovered that life around Heinrich Rosenthal was so full of bustle there wasn't much time left to brood about the past. All around town there were streets he wanted to photograph with his old box camera, from various angles, at various hours of the day; there were angry letters to write to the newspapers; and noisy meetings to conduct of the 'Senior Citizens' Patrol for the Preservation of Jerusalem Landmarks', which he founded himself together with his cronies from the Café Stern. By the way, he wouldn't let me join the patrol because he didn't think anyone under seventy could genuinely appreciate the past, that is in a realistic way, without sentimentalising it.

For all his disapproval of sentimentality, even Mr Rosenthal carried his past around with him in the old grey suitcase. That's where he kept his most cherished possessions.

'When you want to transfer a houseplant from one pot to another,' he explained, 'you have to put a little soil from the old pot in with it. Well, this suitcase is where I keep my soil.'

The only time I had ever seen the suitcase open before was when an old nun from the convent of the Little Sisters of Jesus, the one who speaks fluent Hebrew, came to visit Mr Rosenthal. He opened the suitcase for her and took out an old map with strange markings. But that's a different story, and maybe I'll write about it some day. This time when he opened the suitcase, I saw a stack of papers covered with tiny writing and tied with a string. There was also a thick book with a charred white cover, and a big photograph of a young man in a strange-looking uniform. As he was bending down to close the suitcase I saw an ornate copper box, a gold-plated medallion and a heavy iron pistol. When the suitcase closed again, I was wild with curiosity, though a little disappointed that I'd missed my chance. Now I was going to get another glimpse at the contents of the suitcase, and the eyes that Rudy Schwartz had spoken of.

But he didn't open the suitcase right away. In fact, the suitcase wasn't opened till after their stormy meeting ended, though I didn't realise this at the time. I was busy listening to the two invisible voices.

The enormous black shoes said, 'Listen, Rosenthal, you received my letter, and you know what I want.'

The worn old sneakers said, 'You are very rude, sir, but that I will overlook. In your letter you call me a thief, when we both know who the real thief is. You are the one who stole Edith's heart from me – but that is not what I wish to speak of now.'

Again the shiny shoes spoke up: 'Quite right. What point is there in arguing about something that happened over twenty years ago? Let us speak of the present – where is the mouth? Where is it?'

The sneakers said: 'Rudy, you know very well I would never do such a thing.'

The bully's feet strode across the carpet. Little puffs of dust wafted over me, and I was afraid I would sneeze out loud.

'Listen, Heinrich,' said Rudy Schwartz. 'Yesterday morning I discovered the mouth was missing. That painful picture of her lively, laughing mouth was no longer on the mantle where I've kept it these twenty years.'

'It wasn't me,' blurted Mr Rosenthal. 'It wasn't, I tell you, I – wait! Did you have any unexpected visitors the day before yesterday?'

'I have visitors every day of the week,' said Schwartz, and I noticed his boastful tone. 'Any number of people come to see me, and one of them stole the picture. You sent him to steal it, Rosenthal.'

I couldn't hear Mr Rosenthal's reply, but I imagine he shook his head.

'Who else could it be?'

His scream was so piercing I writhed

under the bed. Schwartz stamped his foot and stepped forward. 'Who else could it be?' he repeated. 'You're the only one who knew I had the portrait of her mouth. You knew because Edith herself told you so when she came to say goodbye and gave you the second picture, the charcoal drawing of her eyes. Those were Edith's last two pictures, Heinrich, and they are not mentioned in any of the books that were written about her. Only you and I know of their existence.'

'But Rudy,' said Mr Rosenthal wearily, 'why would I want to do such a thing?'

There was a moment's pause. Then Schwartz spoke with barely concealed rage.

'Why? For one thing, sir, a hitherto unknown picture by Edith Strauss would fetch millions, as you are very well aware. And the second reason is jealousy. Your jealousy of me. That's right, your morbid jealousy over Edith. Remember?'

He whispered the words cruelly, and I hated him so much that I felt myself tensing, ready to attack.

Again Mr Rosenthal spoke: 'You're making a big mistake, Schwartz,' he said quietly. 'Yes, I have the picture of her eyes, and I cherish it because of my love for Edith, not because of its value on the market. I know that you too loved her, and that the picture is important to you not because of its monetary worth. Knowing that, I would never take it away from you.'

He spoke quietly, controlling his rage, and he was so convincing, I wanted to jump out from under the bed and say to Rudy Schwartz: Can't you see he's telling the truth? Don't you understand that? But of course I didn't move.

'You refuse, then?' said Schwartz, and I felt a cool feather floating up my back. 'Very well, Mr Rosenthal. If we were ordinary men, we would call in the police to settle this. But you and I were students at Heidelberg, and at Heidelberg we had other ways to decide disputes of honour, did we not, Heinrich?'

'What are you talking about?' asked Mr Rosenthal in astonishment.

'Don't play innocent with me, Heinrich. You know exactly what I'm talking about,' answered Schwartz. 'And I suggest we leave strangers out of this. Here in Israel, who would understand?'

'Good God!' said Mr Rosenthal suddenly, and I couldn't for the life of me figure out what they were talking about up there.

'Four o'clock tomorrow afternoon then?' Schwartz suggested coolly.

'But you're mad!' said Mr Rosenthal. 'You're utterly mad! This isn't Heidelberg, you know!'

'Do I detect a note of fear in your voice, Heinrich Rosenthal?' asked Schwartz complacently.

In the silence that followed, I heard Mr Rosenthal breathing hard.

'Excellent,' said the gruff voice. 'Might I suggest the place?'

'By all means,' said Mr Rosenthal faintly.

'The apple orchard outside Kibbutz

Ramat Rachel. True, it's close to the border, but we are not afraid, are we?'

'I see you've thought of everything,' said Mr Rosenthal listlessly.

'Unless you return the picture to me at once,' replied Rudy Schwartz.

Again there was silence, and then the black shoes traced a perfect circle to the door. The door opened and closed behind him, and he quickly walked away. The bed creaked over me as Mr Rosenthal sank down and groaned.

I didn't dare move, cramped though I was, when Mr Rosenthal walked over to the suitcase and opened it. He rummaged around for a moment and took out a picture with a frame. Then he sat heavily down at the table, his back to the room.

I crawled out from under the bed, stood up and shook myself. Mr Rosenthal was sitting perfectly still. At last I saw the gaping suitcase at my feet, revealing its secrets again.

But another sight caught my eye over Mr

Rosenthal's shoulder: the picture he held in his hands.

It was a charcoal drawing of the upper half of a woman's face. A high, broad forehead and thick eyebrows drawn with quick black strokes, and then of course, the eyes. As I stood gazing at them, I was filled with a strange emotion. Perhaps it was sadness, or fear of the unknown. They looked so sombre, so desperate for help. They seemed to gaze right into my eyes, right through to all that lay hidden beyond me, beyond the present, to all that was to be.

## CHAPTER FOUR

# Code of Honour

'Edith Strauss and I met in Jerusalem, twenty-seven years ago,' said Mr Rosenthal. It was a quarter to eight already, and I'd promised to be home by seven, but Mr Rosenthal was so upset I couldn't just leave him there. I went to the kitchenette and fixed a supper of sandwiches, but neither of us was very hungry. Mr Rosenthal chewed on his sandwich lethargically, staring off from time to time and shaking his head in disbelief. 'Has he gone berserk?' he muttered with dismay. 'The savage! Where does he think we are, Germany, half a century ago?'

The grey suitcase was belted shut by now, with the picture of Edith's eyes inside it. I asked Mr Rosenthal to tell me more about

Edith. He didn't feel like talking at first, but grief loosened his tongue. 'Edith left Germany three years before the outbreak of World War II. She was a tall, golden-haired beauty, with eyes – well, you saw for yourself. She had studied art at the academy in Berlin and planned to be a sculptress, but when she arrived in Jerusalem and saw the wild, biblical landscapes, the arched stones in the wadis, the brilliant light and the colour of the hills, she experienced a kind of shock. She gave up sculpture and began to paint. As it happened, she had a fine touch, a wonderful ability to capture the delicate lines of tree and rock.' Mr Rosenthal spoke softly. He gazed off into the distance and ceased to see me. 'She could catch the movement of things,' he said, 'even inanimate things.

'But her success wasn't limited to art,' he said, and began to pace the floor. 'She was very popular too, and so beautiful. Beautiful is too mild a word – she was ravishing with those deep black eyes, her passionate, laughing mouth, her vibrant body. Jerusalem was younger in those days, it bubbled over with newly-arrived artists from Berlin, Vienna, Paris. There were parties every night, dances even the pedantic professors from the Hebrew University came to, lured there by the gaiety – and the drinks!'

Now Mr Rosenthal paced briskly around the room. He was practically shouting, he spoke so loudly, and when he smiled, there was no joy in his eyes. 'Were you an artist too?' I asked.

'Well, not a painter, no. I was a photographer. I wanted to be a painter, but I wasn't talented enough and couldn't support myself at it in those days. It was during the depression. I worked as a house-painter at first, and I washed store windows for a while. There was nothing demeaning about it: we all had to earn a living somehow.' His eyes grew distant. 'Then one day I saw a small ad in the newspaper: Wanted – experienced photographer. Well, Heinrich, I said to myself, you had three years of training in medical photography at the University of Heidelberg. You learned to photograph cells under a microscope; you know how to use all kinds of photographic equipment. Why not take pictures of living people? I scraped some money together and bought myself a box camera, the one you know, the one I use to this day, and then I applied for the job in the paper.'

'And you were hired,' I broke in. It was eight o'clock already and a worried mother and angry father were waiting for me at home.

'No,' smiled Mr Rosenthal, 'I wasn't hired. I had no experience as a news photographer. There I was with my box camera and my empty pockets. I had to do something fast. I went over to the Bezalel Academy and offered my services to the artists on the faculty, but none of them saw any point in having their work photographed, not until I explained how important it was to record the various stages of artistic creation, and to be able to keep a photograph of the paintings they sold. I said a great many things. Hunger enhanced my powers of persuasion. Nobody was especially interested though, until one of the artists decided to hire me, and the rest followed suit, out of jealousy most likely. That's how I came to be an art photographer. And that's how I met Edith too.' He fell silent. He hung his head. It was very disturbing. All his strength seemed to go.

'How dare he call me a miserable thief!' he shouted, waving Schwartz's letter in the air. 'He's the one who stole Edith from me! Me he calls a thief!' His face burned red and his blue eyes popped. I tried to calm him. I told him it was silly to get worked up over something that happened so many years ago, and I brought him a glass of water, but he pushed it away.

I sat down beside him, thinking to myself: Rudy Schwartz is an old man, and so is Mr Rosenthal, however young at heart he may be. That's the only way I can think of them both. But tonight I realised something with a puzzling clarity, something I may have said aloud before but never actually understood: they were all young once upon a time, Mr Rosenthal and Rudy Schwartz, my grandfather and Vera from the antique shop and her husband Avraham. Once upon a time, Mr Rosenthal was a young man who fell in love with Edith and went to dances, certain that the world had been created just for him.

He went on speaking, but I had stopped listening by then. I suddenly felt an urgent need to listen to myself, to the voice within me whispering that even I – at twelve years – was sometimes filled to bursting with energy and joy and excitement that the world was mine, that its tempo and the tempo of everything around me – cars, movies, music, the jokes people told each other and the advertisements we heard – kept perfect time with my own tempo, the tempo of my teens. And at such moments I couldn't understand the Rosenthals and

Schwartzes of this world nor any of the grown-ups who'd lived before me, who'd lived life with the same intense delight before the tempo speeded up so much they had to drop out; and maybe someday I would have children and grandchildren of my own who would find it hard to believe that I was ever young and in love with life. But suddenly, in the midst of my euphoria, I remembered Mom telling me that sometimes I act like an old man; and once I overheard her telling Dad that I don't really know how to enjoy life. These thoughts confused me. I suddenly felt angry and restless. That's why I stood up.

Mr Rosenthal was so startled he stopped talking in mid-sentence. For a moment we looked at each other in silence, and then I said, 'Mr Rosenthal, I get as much pleasure from reading books as other people do from playing soccer or going to parties, and she doesn't know anything. You don't live in the past. You enjoy each moment your own way, and that's exactly what I intend to do. My own way. And when I grow up, I'm going to write books. I have big plans, and I don't think that if . . .'

I don't know why I was saying all this, why I was talking such nonsense. I just felt that if I didn't say it out loud to someone, I'd go nuts. Mr Rosenthal looked at me and smiled. He put his hand on my shoulder. I could see he was worried, but even at a time like this he had a smile for me. 'It's all my fault,' he said. 'I shouldn't have mixed you up in all this, in my problems with Schwartz, that terrible savage. Now go home, friend David. It's late. And your mother – it was your mother you were speaking of, I believe? We'll talk about that another time, tomorrow or maybe the day after. If we should be so fortunate.'

I was all confused and angry with myself, and didn't pay much attention to those last words of his. It was only later on my way home in the cold Jerusalem night – after managing somehow (it took three tries) to put my sweater on right side out and to come up with a good excuse to give my parents for being late – that they finally sank in. 'We'll talk about that another time, tomorrow or maybe the day after. If we should be so fortunate.' What a strange thing to say, I mused. It isn't like him. I stood still a moment. Something dawned on me and gave me a fright. I swerved around and ran all the way back to the Beit Hakerem Home for the Aged. The entrance gate was locked, but I saw the watchman sitting in the lobby. He knew me. Everyone there knew me because I spent so much time with Mr Rosenthal. 'Kind of late for a visit,' said the watchman, unlocking the door for me. I tossed him some sort of reply and hurried up to the second floor.

I walked right into Mr Rosenthal's room without knocking and much to my amazement, found him sitting on his bed, cleaning something with a fine brush. There were several hunks of metal beside him on the bed. He looked up at me, and before he could open his mouth I asked, 'What's all this?'

'This? This is my gun. It's my old service pistol from the World War I.' He chuckled as he continued to clean it with the brush.

'What do you need a gun for?' I asked in horror.

He looked at me and smiled. 'You didn't understand, did you? You didn't understand what Schwartz was talking about?' I shook my head.

Again he smiled, a sad and bitter smile. He raised the piece of metal and looked at it in the light.

'Schwartz thinks we're back in the old days in Germany,' he grumbled. 'And because he called me a thief and a coward, I must submit to the old code of honour, however absurd it may seem today!'

'What on earth are you talking about, Mr Rosenthal?' I asked quietly, though I had already begun to guess.

He gave me a strange, penetrating look.

'Schwartz has challenged me to a duel at four o'clock tomorrow, and though it may seem insane, I feel I have no choice but to accept.' He gazed at me, troubled and helpless. Slowing he spread his hands in a gesture of despair.

## CHAPTER FIVE

# Times Change

I didn't get much sleep that night.

First my parents bawled me out for getting home at nine o'clock in the evening instead of seven; actually I claimed it was nine o'clock in the evening and they insisted it was nine o'clock at night. Anyway, this minor difference of opinion resulted in a fight.

Mom said I was not permitted to visit Mr Rosenthal anymore, and that tomorrow we would begin an intensive programme to tighten any screws that had come loose as a result of my rubbing against unsuitable company. Dad on the other hand confined himself to a few remarks: a) he respected me for having such a rich inner life; and b) though I certainly seemed to enjoy a variety of exciting activities, he thought I might be shutting myself off a bit too much; and while he was well aware of the courage it took to maintain my privacy and independence in this intrusive world of ours, I would have to exhibit a different kind of daring and start connecting with people my own age. He's a lawyer, my dad.

This really made me mad. They were talking as if I didn't have enough confidence to make friends of my own age, as if I'd never had friends in life. Right there I gave them a list of my friends and hoped that would put an end to the argument, only Mom refused to admit that one name constitutes a list, especially when it belongs to someone who moved to Haifa six months ago and who stays in touch by mail; 'Mighty peculiar mail at that,' she added, not that she ever read his letters but, heaven forbid, she simply couldn't fail to observe my reaction when I read them.

I told her Elisha's letters weren't peculiar at all, they were hilarious. He had the zaniest ideas and he really knew how to crack me up. I also said that someday when he grew up and people read his stories, Elisha would be very famous, and she and Dad would be proud of their son for knowing him.

Dad, who was making coffee in the kitchen just then, shouted from there that he hoped they would be proud of their own son first.

I couldn't stand them when they talked like that, so I went off to my room to simmer for a while. I took Bugs Bunny out of his cage, scratched his back the way he likes, and whispered certain unrepeatable things into his long ears, because I knew that he could keep a secret.

At this point I'd like to make a short digression for a bit of meanness. Elisha is twenty-eight years old today, and he's a writer like me. I just love it when Mom, who's interested in literature, says that he definitely has a future and that some day we'll be proud to know him. I never remind her of those 'discussions' we used to have, but I can hardly refrain from saying I told you so.

So much for Elisha and the argument.

I sat on my bed in the dark, stroking Bugs Bunny and trying to calm down. His smooth white fur crackled with electricity when I touched him. I was trying to remember the things Mr Rosenthal had said an hour before: Schwartz was so sure he'd stolen the picture of Edith's mouth that he challenged him to a pistol duel. Mr Rosenthal knew he hadn't stolen the picture, yet he couldn't ignore being called 'a miserable thief and a coward.' It was very perplexing: Mr Rosenthal himself had said he was ashamed of accepting Schwartz's ridiculous challenge to meet him in the apple orchard the following day.

'Those foolish, bombastic notions of "honour or death" belong to an era long ago. The world was more honourable in the old days, if a little theatrical for my liking. There was room then for words like "honour" and "pride", something I can't say about the world today. If Schwartz had called me a liar back in our youth, I would have sent a friend posthaste to tell him only blood would avenge his insult.'

'And what then?' I asked.

'What then?' He stretched in his chair. 'The friend would have waited for Schwartz's written consent to duel with me. Of course, Schwartz might have chosen to apologise instead, in which case the duel would have been cancelled, only then he would have proven himself a coward, which in those days was an anathema – not like today, when it's practically the style.'

'I didn't know Jews fought duels,' I said.

'Ho ho,' laughed Mr Rosenthal. 'At the turn of the century, the anti-Semitic students in Germany banned us from their duelling societies, so we Jews founded societies of our own to prove we were as good as the Germans. Even I fought a few duels in my day, though fortunately, no one was ever hurt.'

'How do you fight a duel?' I asked.

'Ah! It's a solemn ritual. You meet on the duelling grounds with your seconds, have something to eat or drink and shake hands, while a third party inspects the weapons. Then, at a signal from him, you each take five paces, turn around, and shoot.'

'Just like that? You shoot each other?' My voice suddenly sounded like a high pitched squeal.

When Mr Rosenthal saw the look of shock on my face, he smiled wearily and said, 'Yes, yes, friend David. You shoot. In those days people were less concerned about life than they were about honour. One of the duellers was usually wounded, though sometimes both were killed. And all on account of an insult, or the barest suspicion of an insult. It's hard to believe, isn't it?'

Mr Rosenthal himself is about to do the same ridiculous thing tomorrow, I thought to myself, and said nothing.

'Ah me,' he sighed. 'When honour

becomes so important, a man will stop at nothing to defend it.' Then he laughed. 'How absurd it is, two grown men shooting each other over a word! What waste! What dishonour to the human race!'

He was silent a moment and then spoke the words I had just been thinking: 'And tomorrow I myself am going to play this senseless game. It's simply unbelievable.'

I tried to talk him out of it, to persuade him to forget this childish idea. I begged him to send Schwartz a letter calling off the duel. I even offered to write to Schwartz myself. But he was unmoved. 'What would you write, then, friend David?' he laughed. ' "Dear Mr Schwartz, little Heinrich will not be able to attend your duel tomorrow because he is afraid."? Oh no, that will not do. Not this time. Do you understand? It isn't just the matter of Edith's picture. Rudy Schwartz and I have a little unfinished business to settle, another hurt or two. The duel must take place.' And after a moment's pause he said something that really took me by surprise: 'We come from different generations, you and I. I know that Schwartz is utterly mad, but at the same time, in some irrational way, I can't help sympathising with him. I understand him. For you that may be difficult to grasp. You see, friend David, the world is changing. It changes so quickly. What was good yesterday is bad today, what was beautiful once is ugly now. Fashions fade with such tedious regularity. Rudy Schwartz cannot adapt to the changing world, so he defends himself against it with the only weapon he has. He stops himself and starts up again at a different pace. He reverts to the world of long ago. You don't know what I'm talking about, do you? But you will one day, much as I hate to say it.'

He put his hand on my shoulder and walked me to the door. He wanted to be alone now. Before we said goodbye he told me that he couldn't bring himself to hate Schwartz. 'Oddly enough,' he said, 'I'm unable to hate the man.'

Those were his parting words to me before I dashed off to my warm home and the cold shower awaiting me there. But later, as I sat on my bed holding good old Bugsy, I realised there was some truth to what he said; the world is changing so fast there aren't many things you can rely on, and even fewer people. What was certain, though, was that life is more important than anything, even honour, which I don't quite understand in any case; and even a million years from now there will be some things people can rely on. But this wasn't the time to drown in thought, because I had to come up with a plan to rescue Mr Rosenthal from the bully of Heidelberg – though it looked as if I might have to do it single-handedly, now that Mr Rosenthal had resigned himself to the idea of the duel. So I got myself ready for bed and lay down to sleep, hungry and miserable. I couldn't stop thinking that a few hours from now Heinrich Rosenthal and Rudy Schwartz would be facing each other at ten paces; and though the duel would be taking place in a little apple orchard in Jerusalem, not the forests of Germany, both men would be holding real guns in their hands with real bullets in them. Which is why I barely slept a wink that night.

## CHAPTER SIX

# Here's the story of Vera

When Vera was a young woman, her husband Avraham joined the British Army and was sent away to the Libyan desert to fight the Germans. Avraham, who was a doctor, refused to sit around twiddling his thumbs when every man was needed in the war against the Nazi Beast. The 'Nazi Beast' is what they used to call the Germans. When I was a kid, I honestly thought they were talking about some real animal. I imagined it as a kind of monster or giant dinosaur the whole world had to fight. Anyway, Vera's husband was sent away, and one month later she received a letter from him. He was stationed in a village on the border between Egypt, Libya, and Sudan, where the nights were cold and food was scarce. He said he was lonely for her. They'd been married barely a year, and Vera missed him so much she decided to go out to join him in the desert. I must have heard this story twenty times, but I still enjoy hearing it. Vera was like delicate china, but she tried not to think about the hardships waiting for her in the desert. She took the train from Jerusalem, and after an exhausting trip, arrived in Cairo, where she switched to the bumpy night train, the only woman in the crowd. The next morning, the train stopped somewhere along the Nile, and Vera Kluger, wearing two sweaters, a fur coat and a woollen scarf because Avraham had written how cold it got out there at night, stepped off and sank up to her knees in the burning sand. I can just imagine her: the pale young woman wearing a fur coat, sinking in the golden sand. From there she took a rickety boat down the Nile, and as it floated past the giant temples, she had to fight off a young thief who tried to steal her necklace and a particularly nasty swarm of green flies. The next lap of the journey was by 'felucca', a local fishing boat, and finally, a two day ride on a grumpy camel to the border village where Avraham's camp was. She found him burning up with some rare desert fever, and he thought he must be delirious when he saw Vera there.

After the war, Vera and Avraham bought a house in the Beit Hakerem neighbourhood. Avraham opened his clinic, and Vera, who wanted to be more than 'the doctor's wife', opened an antique shop.

And it was to Vera's antique shop that I hurried the morning of the duel.

When I got there at twenty to eight, she was standing in the semi-darkness drinking tea from a glass. The smoke from her cigarette floated around her like a permanent cloud. She was startled to see me: 'What is it, *mein kind*? So early in the morning? Is everything all right at home?'

'Everything's all right,' I said. 'Don't worry, Vera, no one's sick.' I recognised each item in the darkened shop: the samovars, the wooden table lamps, the big pictures in gilded frames, the piles of old postcards, the fancy outfits people wore in Jerusalem thirty and forty years ago – it was a different world in Vera's shop. Customers used to come from all over the city to sell Vera the junk they found in their attics, only the trouble was, none of them came in to buy, though Vera didn't really mind much, because she was happy just to chat. I used to spend hours in the shop with her, which, as you can probably imagine, was another thing that infuriated my mom.

Only this time it wasn't Vera's antiques I was interested in but her no less antique memories.

Time was running out, and I got straight to the point. I asked her to promise not to ask any questions. She might have refused, of course, but I knew she was curious, and sure enough, her eyes began to twinkle slyly behind her gold-framed glasses. 'Yes,' she promised. Secrets she likes.

'Did you know the artist Edith Strauss?'

She stared at me in astonishment. She hadn't expected a question like that.

'Sure I knew Edith, a long time ago, though, back in the forties, I think. We even spoke once or twice. But why are you . . . ? Okay, I promised not to ask questions. What exactly do you want to know about her?'

'Everything,' I said, glancing at my watch. It was a quarter to eight. It would take me two minutes to run to school. My gamble that Vera knew something about Edith had paid off. Now I had to get all the information I could to help me figure out what to do.

'Everything,' I repeated. Vera looked into my eyes. She could see how important this was to me, and began to speak.

'Edith came from Germany. She was a beautiful woman, and everyone was in love with her. I think there's a picture of her in the encyclopaedia. She was a very great artist. Her paintings are worth millions today. It's sad that she didn't paint more before she died.' Vera considered a moment, looked at me sideways, and went on. 'Edith was moody, temperamental. She drank too much, and after weeks of frenzied love she would fall into terrible depressions. Maybe all great artists suffer like that, but as far as I'm concerned, she was just a very sick, unhappy woman who could only fall in love, but didn't really know how to love, if you know what I mean. Oh wait!' Vera peered at me over her glasses. 'That friend of yours, you know, the nice old gentleman you brought in here once, Rosenberg? Rosenbloom? Rosenthal! Right, he was one of her friends. And what a romance that was! It was the talk of the town! He was a photographer, I believe, or was he a poet? He and Edith fell madly in love at first sight, but it ended just as suddenly for some reason. Edith never had reasons, only moods. Then she went off with a British officer who was stationed here during the Mandate period, and –'

'A British officer?' I asked. 'Not

Schwartz?'

'Schwartz?' said Vera, trying to recall. 'She had so many beaux, there may have been one named Schwartz, I don't know. But the Englishman was the one she married, and there was a very big to-do about that.' Vera paused. She didn't really know what happened later. She had lost track of the gossip when she met her Avraham and stopped mixing in Bohemian circles.

I asked her what the British officer's name was but she didn't know.

'It was a strange affair,' she said. 'In those days girls who socialised with British soldiers were condemned, and sometimes punished by the Resistance. They threatened Edith too, but she ignored them till one day – one night, really – when she came home, she found them waiting for her. They tied her up and shaved her head as a sign of disgrace.'

Vera stared through me. 'All that wavy golden hair,' she said. 'They shaved it off.

She was in shock, the poor girl. She couldn't understand why they'd done such a thing to her. She said she had to leave, she couldn't stand it here any more, she would never be able to paint in a country where people treated each other that way. And a few weeks later she left for England, where she married her British officer, and I heard they had a baby girl, or maybe it was a boy? Anyway, shortly after, Edith died. That was over twenty years ago. But tell me, why are you so interested in her?'

'Vera, you promised,' I said. 'Don't worry though, I'll tell you soon enough.' And I ran off to school.

It was almost eight now and I had only eight hours left to straighten out the awful mess, which by this time involved three countries, Germany, Israel and England, several love affairs, a stolen picture worth millions, and most alarming of all – two pistols from World War I.

## CHAPTER SEVEN

# The Story of their Love

It was eight o'clock when I entered the classroom and by five past I was out of there. To make a long story short, Mr Levine the English teacher zeroed in on me the minute he walked in. Levine was always giving me a hard time. The trouble was, he was psychic, and knew just when to call on me. Why he ignored me every time I came in prepared, God alone can say, but He never does.

So there I was out in the hall with a vague warning about what to expect if I didn't mend my (English) ways, and a more substantial punishment – to write a five page composition, in English, about 'A Day in the Life of George, the Boy from London'.

But I had no time for George the city boy, nor did I regret being thrown out of class, because, as you may recall, time was running out, and unless I thought of something fast – there would be bloodshed.

That's why I hurried upstairs to the school library. I wanted to look up Edith Strauss in the encyclopaedia, but the 'S' volume only went up to 'Scythians, a fierce nomadic people from south-eastern Europe and Asia', and the next volume was gone, so I thumbed through a book about modern Jewish art instead – and bingo, I found her. Quickly I scanned the page: 'Strauss, Edith. Born – 1918, Berlin; died – 1949, England . . . unique style . . . deeply embedded in European culture . . . merged with the reality and disposition of Palestine . . . dynamic . . . well-known series of paintings called "Israel and the Desert" . . . temperamental . . . scandal of a love affair with an officer of the British Mandate led to her departure . . . towards the end of her life, embittered against Israel and Judaism . . . died in the resort town of Brighton . . . paintings highly valued by collectors and museums alike (*see* picture overleaf).'

I turned the page and there for the first time, saw Edith Strauss. She really was fabulous looking. Her eyes, deep and black, were the eyes I had seen the day before in Mr Rosenthal's picture. She wore a wide-brimmed hat with a feather in it over the beautiful wavy hair the Resistance had shaved off as a mark of disgrace. I studied the tall figure of Edith Strauss in a long dress and clumsy-looking shoes. I tried to understand the spell she had cast over everyone who knew her, the magic that was prompting two old men to fight a duel over a self-portrait she had drawn, twenty years after her death. I didn't understand it – I have to admit – but my long look at the picture eventually paid off. More about that later.

I shut the book and stared out the window. Autumn was fighting for its life out there, trying to disarm the menacing winter with flights of yellow leaves and feather clouds. The rainy season hadn't started yet. I tried to concentrate. Everything had started to seem so strange and unpredictable when I read Schwartz's letter to Mr Rosenthal the day before: I was suddenly living in a different time zone, in a different country: I had been hurled out of my normal life into another reality, a reality that had its own rules and its own sensations.

But then, still drowning in thought, I happened to catch sight of little Mr Rosenthal standing outside in front of the school. I ran out to him.

He wasn't there by chance. He'd come to say goodbye. The realisation hit me hard, like a punch in the belly. We walked a little way together. He was wearing a heavy coat and a cap that hid his eyes. The wind blew in my face. The sky turned grey.

'I'm saying my farewells to Jerusalem,' he said in a quiet monotone. 'I'm making the rounds of the houses and the rented rooms I've lived in during my thirty years in this city, taking a last look at every street corner I ever photographed.' He like to photograph old houses, as I mentioned before.

'Maybe it's not farewell for ever,' I suggested in a half-whisper.

'No, no,' said Mr Rosenthal. 'One or the other of us will be shot, and if it's Schwartz, my life won't be worth living anyway.'

I knew it. Mr Rosenthal wouldn't hurt a fly, which is why he wore sneakers instead of leather shoes, and had been a strict vegetarian for forty years.

'Maybe you'll both miss,' I said.

'Well, I hope so,' he replied. 'But don't forget, Schwartz was an expert marksman in his day.'

'That was fifty years ago,' I reminded him.

'Yes,' he said. 'but rage will sharpen his senses. Come, friend David, let's walk on.'

Slowly we strolled down the path to the Valley of Zion, between the tall, bald thistles left over from summer. There was a feeling of anticipation in the air. A strong wind blew us the news of big clouds carrying rain. The cypress trees murmured low, and flurries of yellow leaves swirled through the air.

'For a year and a half we lived together, Edith and I,' said Mr Rosenthal. He climbed up on a big rock and sat dangling his legs like a little boy on a bus bench. I sat down beside him. 'We were very happy together, and very unhappy too,' he continued. 'We loved each other so much, yet we fought constantly. We were too much alike and too different. It was an impossible relationship. She was a loner. Even when she was surrounded by people she felt alone. Do you understand anything I'm saying?'

Yes I understood.

'She was happy with me, but she said my love was suffocating her; that her love for me was hurting her, changing her, keeping her from being free. And she couldn't stand it.'

He fell silent, and rubbed a few leaves of sage between his fingers. He inhaled with pleasure, I noticed.

'And then Rudy came on the scene,' he said. 'Rudy Schwartz, whom I had known in Heidelberg. He was tall and handsome, strong as an ox, an excellent dancer too, and,' he added with quiet bitterness, 'a great fool. Edith fell passionately in love with him.' Pensive grey clouds blew in from the east. Mr Rosenthal tried to control his voice. 'She said that with Schwartz she could escape from herself and the fears that so tormented her. How jealous I was when I saw them dancing together at the art school ball or drinking in the fashionable cafés. I would glance at them and weep inwardly. I could see that Edith was deteriorating. Her eyes had a strange glint. The paintings she produced during that period, paintings you can see today in museums all over the world, had something distorted about them, something unhealthy.' He sighed. I looked anxiously up at the sky which was darkening over. 'Her condition was growing worse and worse,' continued Mr Rosenthal. 'She broke off with Schwartz and fell in love with another man, and after him, with another. She lived in perpetual motion, in perpetual flight. In the end she met a British officer and left the country full of bitterness.' He sighed and adjusted his cap. 'People were very cruel to her,' he said. 'But I don't want to talk about that now.

'She came to say goodbye before she left. Poor woman, she looked like a burned out candle and she was seriously ill. In parting she gave me her latest sketch, the portrait of her eyes. She told me she had given the one of her mouth to Schwartz. "The eyes are yours because you have seen into me," she said, "You have seen the real Edith. And to him I gave my mouth, my laughter and my kisses. Between you now you have all of Edith." '

Mr Rosenthal sighed and went on in a quiet, distant voice.

'When she stood up to leave, she touched me between the eyes. Her finger was so hot, I felt as if I had been burned. That was more than twenty years ago. Then she said, "These two portraits are my last, Heinrich. I can't paint anymore." And I stood before her with my eyes closed, and my forehead still burning where her finger had touched me. When I looked up, Edith was gone.'

Slowly he shook his head. The old memories weighed heavily upon him. All of a sudden, the first rain began to fall.

## CHAPTER EIGHT

# Goodbye, Mr Rosenthal

It was twelve o'clock, two hours since Mr Rosenthal and I had said our goodbyes. I'd never said goodbye like that to anyone before. When Elisha moved to Haifa, I knew he'd be coming back to visit and that we'd be able to write to each other. But here I was saying goodbye for ever to someone who was about to die. It was inconceivable. Rain fell as we sat on our rock in the Valley of Zion facing Beit Hakerem. Mr Rosenthal breathed in the moist air and said, 'Ah, the first rain.' But I was thinking – you know what I was thinking.

It was no use trying to convince him to give up about the silly duel. It was no use trying to make him see that we were living in Jerusalem in 1966, because he knew that as well as I did. Only yesterday after Rudy Schwartz's visit he himself had said, 'That savage, he must think he's in Germany at the turn of the century!' But I knew it was too late to change anything. Schwartz had challenged him to a duel, and he couldn't back down now. 'I'll be a laughing-stock if I do,' he insisted. 'Everyone will ridicule me.' By everyone he meant his cronies from Café Stern, his fellow members in the Senior Citizens Patrol for the Preservation of Jerusalem Landmarks.

And then I noticed he was more dressed-up than usual. He had on a chequered jacket, a white shirt and black trousers under his coat, though he was still wearing his old sneakers. I told him he looked nice, and he smiled sadly. He said he'd pulled out his entire wardrobe for the occasion. 'Since I'm about to take leave of my senses,' he said, 'and go back half a century in time, I may as well do it in style.' And leaning toward me he added with a strange chuckle, 'Yes, I'm even planning to put a red rose in my lapel.'

Then I started thinking that maybe the idea of a duel and returning to his youth had gotten to him, maybe he was starting to like it. But I said nothing. All of a sudden he blared in a voice that was not his own, 'Pushkin, the great Russian poet was killed in a duel. It's a very distinguished way to die, I'll have you know.'

It isn't the least bit distinguished, I thought, but still said nothing. Now I knew he was far away, in a different place and time, and I felt sadder than ever.

But then he said something strange. 'Well, at least my conscience will be clear.'

'What do you mean?' I asked him.

He opened the box he was carrying and took out a gun – the steel grey pistol he kept in the suitcase in his room. He picked it up in both hands and aimed it at the branches of the pine tree in the wadi. There were two sparrows perched there, sheltering from the rain. Mr Rosenthal closed one eye and pressed the trigger.

I shut my eyes in terror. Something was definitely wrong with Mr Rosenthal. I trembled when I heard the shot. It reverberated ominously through the hills. I opened my eyes. The two sparrows were still perched on the branch. Mr Rosenthal looked at me and laughed. The gun in his hand wasn't smoking. The shot I'd thought I heard had been no more than the rumbling of thunder.

'I do not intend to use bullets,' said Mr Rosenthal. 'I've thrown them all away.'

I stared at him bewilderedly: 'But Mr Rosenthal, Schwartz's gun will be loaded!'

'Mine will not. That way I can keep a clean conscience and also my pride. I will fight the duel – but I will not hurt anyone. I have never in my life shed blood, and I don't intend to start now.' I looked at him and said nothing. What is he doing? I thought to myself. I know I wouldn't show up to a duel without a loaded gun, plus a sword, just to be on the safe side. But then I thought, what for? What would Mr Rosenthal gain by hurting Schwartz? Revenge? How stupid it all was. 'Friend David,' said Mr Rosenthal, 'I want you to know how deeply I appreciate your saying nothing just now. Thank you for not trying to convince me to load my pistol for the duel.' He took a deep breath, looked me in the eye and said: 'Listen, there are a few matters left that need attention, and I'm counting on your help.'

I could hardly see anymore with the tears and the rain in my eyes, but I gazed steadily ahead. Mr Rosenthal handed me the keys to his room and asked me to return them to Mr Toussia at the Home, if the worst came to the worst. He had already straightened out financial matters in the office, he said, so I needn't bother about that. The more complicated things would be looked after by his friends from Café Stern. He had made all the necessary arrangements, but he had one request of me: the suitcase, the grey suitcase in his room. Would I get rid of it somehow? It contained nothing of any real value, except sentimental value, so I should take whatever I wished for myself, and get rid of the rest.

Suddenly I had an idea. Why hadn't I thought of it sooner? Would he mind, I asked, if I took what was left in the suitcase to Vera's antique shop? Mr Rosenthal remembered Vera. I had brought him to her shop once and shown him around. Mr Rosenthal had said he wasn't especially fond of old junk that was only good for nostalgia. But I could see that he liked Vera, and they drank tea and chatted together for a long time. Naturally she told him about her journey on the Nile, and he laughed like a kid. Then they talked about the state of the world and their plans for the future. Hey, I thought to myself, too bad Vera already has a husband or I could fix the two of them up, the way they do in the movies.

When I mentioned Vera to him he was pleased. He said that would be the perfect way to dispense with the suitcase, and that if Vera happened to sell any of the contents, he would be glad his memories were good for something after all.

Then he got up and shook my hand and asked me not to follow. He turned and walked away. Just like that. I stayed on the rock, sopping wet and sick of the world. Gradually he disappeared up the path, his sneakers soaked with mud. It was a long time before I ambled off and wandered aimlessly through the streets in the pouring rain.

It was one o'clock by the time I arrived at the Home in Beit Hakerem. The old people were sitting around the lobby the way they always did. Some were staring into space and some were talking to each other or muttering to themselves. It was very quiet. I went up to the second floor and into Mr Rosenthal's room. It was strange to be there without him. The room looked completely different somehow, even though everything was in its place. I looked around and felt a terrible pang: I had spent so many hours in this room. I had met so many of his friends here – the friends he collected, as he put it, like some people collect stamps. Now all that was over.

Under the table I saw the small, grey suitcase he'd brought from Germany, where his memories were stored.

I crouched down and opened it. Before me lay stacks of paper, books and various possessions. Just then I had a thought, and then another thought. First, the famous portrait of the eyes was still inside the suitcase. And second, and a lot more frighteningly: whoever stole Schwartz's picture might also steal Mr Rosenthal's!

The thought was so alarming that I froze in midair over the suitcase. But I didn't stay that way for long, because just then I heard the muffled scurrying of feet in the hallway. The footsteps stopped outside the room. My heart was pounding as someone tried the lock and then decided to push the handle – and the door opened wide.

## CHAPTER NINE

# Reflections of a Junior Sleuth

Now I want to talk about happy things, like
the letters Elisha sends me from Heifa, or
the play we made up together last year –
where the words were all written backwards, and the plot was backwards too – or
like – oh anything, anything whatever, just
so I don't have to tell about the terror that
gripped me as the footsteps in the corridor
drew near and the handle turned and the
door creaked open. At that moment I flew –
there's no other way to explain what happened – but literally flew past the chair on
my right, hovered in mid air over the wastebasket and flitted round the room, swift
and silent as a bat, till I chanced on the
best hideout I could possibly have found,
the big wardrobe into which I disappeared,

shutting the panel behind me before I heard the door close softly, and the stranger was inside.

There are times in life when a person thinks with the intensity of three minds: one mind plans a daring strategy, the second cancels it, and the third quakes with fear and hums a little song of defeat. Inside the darkened wardrobe I was entirely under the control of mind number three, and all I could hear was the tune of defeat. There was another sound too though: the uneasy pattering of the stranger's feet around the room. I heard a desk drawer open and there was silence. The rustling of paper. The drawer closed. More footsteps. I leaned back in the wardrobe and smelled the moth-balls and the sage Mr Rosenthal put there to make his clothes smell fresh and good. I tried to hide among the suits and shirts, the flannel trousers and the woollen vests, pretending to be a coat myself, something with hooks and buttons, to avoid being a live, scared, thinking individual.

The closet door was open a crack. I didn't have time to shut it all the way when the supernatural forces were whisking me in there. The thin strip of light that filtered through, obscured my vision of the room. But to tell the truth, I didn't much care what was happening in the room; all I wanted was for whatever it was to stop happening so that I could come out of my suffocating hideaway.

Here's something worth thinking about: I used to spend so much time lying under the covers in my room at home with Bugs Bunny, day-dreaming about the brave feats I would perform someday in situations like the one I was in right now. I would imagine myself boldly leaping out at some thief and/or pirate and/or killer, surprising him from behind with a double-nelson and punching him in the chin with a fist of iron, then helping him up on his wobbly legs and putting a pair of shiny handcuffs around his wrists, saying coolly: 'Okay, Jonny, the game is up.' Yet despite so many hours of day-dreaming practice, when the moment came, I lost my nerve. I was so scared I didn't even try to peek out at the stranger – an offence that would no doubt have got me expelled from any reputable school for sleuths, or at best, the report card they gave me would have read something like, 'promoted, but not in our school'.

Whoever was prowling around out there certainly didn't waste any time on fear and trepidation. In fact, he seemed to be very confident: I heard his lively footsteps and then the effortful breathing as he crouched down, presumably, to look under the bed, and his truly amazing energy in opening and shutting drawers in quick succession. I was sure that a few minutes from now he would search through the closet, and I wasn't exactly thrilled at the prospect. But I had one basis for hope: the way I figured it, this thief was bound to get jumpy and want to take off from the scene of the crime, even if he hadn't finished doing the job yet. Carefully I raised my hand and brought my watch close to my eyes. It glowed green in the darkness: ten minutes to two. If the thief got out of here fast enough, I would be able to make it to kibbutz Ramat Rachel in time to tell Mr Rosenthal and Rudy Schwartz that I had seen the thief, or at least that I knew a thief existed; or at any rate, that there was a third person involved who knew about the pictures Edith Strauss had given them before she left the country; and this meant that instead of duelling, they ought to be teaming up to catch the thief.

But then another idea struck me, one so dazzling I could already imagine the principal of the school for sleuths pleading with my father to let me re-enrol, not as an ordinary student, but as an instructor of up-and-coming sleuths.

And here's the idea I had: besides me, no one but Mr Rosenthal and Rudy Schwartz knew about the two pictures. Now Schwartz knew that Mr Rosenthal was on his way to the apple orchard at Ramat Rachel. So what would prevent him from searching Mr Rosenthal's room for his picture, which he believed to be there?

And then I added yet another brilliant idea to my chain of mental feats: maybe Schwartz was just a liar? Maybe the whole thing was a trick to get Mr Rosenthal out of his room at a certain time so that Schwartz could go in there unchecked and steal the picture that rightfully belonged to Mr Rosenthal!

I do hope you follow my line of reasoning. Anyone who's ever read a detective book will have no trouble understanding. I for one, understood perfectly well; in fact, the more I understood, the angrier I became. That's demonic, I thought to myself, my fists clenching with rage. That Rudy Schwartz has the mind of a fiend! He sends Mr Rosenthal a threatening letter accusing him of breaking into his home and stealing the picture of the mouth, when in fact the picture was never stolen at all; the whole stupid duel was only a ploy to help Rudy Schwartz steal the picture of Edith's eyes from Mr Rosenthal's room!

Just then my fears departed. I remembered Mr Rosenthal's distress that morning, and the way he had mentally taken leave of all that was dear to him. I knew that what Rudy Schwartz had done was unforgivably cruel. Sweat bubbled up in the palms of my hands and I felt fury shoot out like two red horns on my brow. Any minute I might butt them against the wardrobe! What did I care that Rudy Schwartz wore a size 17 shoe, that he was once known as the bully of Heidelberg, and that he might be packing a pistol from World War I? I knew I had to do something, if only to get even with him for terrifying Mr Rosenthal. So without a second thought – which is pretty untypical of me, as you've probably noticed by now – I cleared my way through the shirts and coats and trousers, then pushed the door open – and jumped out.

And the prowler, who was leaning over the suitcase just then, leaped up like a frightened cat and banged into the bed.

Face to face, we both let out a scream. We screamed because we were startled of course – but I was even more startled to discover how familiar the stranger's face was. Just that morning I had sat gazing at a picture of it in the school library. I wasn't mistaken. The stranger standing before me in Heinrich Rosenthal's room at the Home for the Aged was not Rudy Schwartz at all, but a beautiful young woman; she was, fantastically enough, none other than Edith Strauss the artist, who had died seventeen years before in Brighton, England.

## CHAPTER TEN

# Ann

I screamed. I don't remember whether I screamed 'Yipes!' or 'Help!' or 'Mommy!'. I only know it was a blood-curdling scream of fear: there I was, face to face with the ghost, the ghost of Edith Strauss.

'Oh God!' said the ghost in fluent English.

Neither of us moved. She was a little taller than me, and in spite of the tremendous glasses that covered half her face I saw exactly who she was. That very morning, as you may recall, Mr Levine had sent me out of English class to write a composition, instead of which I had gone upstairs to the school library and come across a picture of Edith Strauss in a book on modern Jewish art, together with the information that

Edith Strauss had died in Brighton, England in 1949. Mr Rosenthal and Vera both confirmed the fact, so there was no reason to doubt it. Besides, if Edith Strauss were still alive by some miracle, she would have to be fifty years old, while the woman before me didn't appear to be more than twenty, in her blue-jean overalls and 'mod' glasses, hardly the uniform of the college of ghosts.

But aside of this minor discrepancy, she was the image of Edith, no mistake about it. The trouble was, mistakes I could handle, ghosts were a different story.

'You look so pale,' said the worried ghost in heavily accented Hebrew. She took a handkerchief out of her pocket, moistened it in the sink across the room and began to rub my forehead. 'Come, sit here. You'll feel better soon,' she said. Her hand smelled sweet like perfume, and she had a soft sort of curious expression on her face. A nice variety of ghost, I decided.

'My name is Ann,' she said, 'Ann Strauss.'

'And I'm a real jerk,' I said. She looked at me curiously. I heaved a sigh.

'My name is David. And you must be the daughter of Edith Strauss, right?'

'But how do you know about my mother?'

'I've heard quite a lot about her in the past twenty-four hours.'

If only I had paid closer attention to what Vera was saying that morning, I might have saved myself a bad scare and guessed that Ann was Edith's daughter, not her ghost – even though Vera wasn't sure whether Edith had given birth to a boy or a girl. But then I remembered that Ann owed me a couple of explanations. I stood up and told her that there were a few things she didn't know, there we were in the middle of a life or death emergency, and that unless she told me everything about the stolen picture, unless she explained right away what she was doing in Mr Rosenthal's room, there would be serious trouble. I talked so fast I don't think she understood all the words I said, but the urgency of my voice convinced her to tell me what she knew.

She was four years old when her mother died. She had only the dimmest memories of Edith, who spent her last years in a sanatorium. Ann had been raised by her father and his second wife, who was a kind and loving stepmother. Her father never spoke about Edith's life so Ann hadn't even suspected that she was Jewish or felt any special tie with Israel.

But three years ago her father died, leaving Ann a letter Edith had written to her before she passed away. Ann paused in her story, trying to decide whether or not I was old enough to understand. I looked her right in the eye. She went on.

In her letter Edith asked her daughter's forgiveness. She reproached herself for failing Ann as a mother and for leaving her at such a tender age. 'By the time you read this,' she wrote, 'you will be quite a grown-up lady, perhaps with children of your own.' She spoke about her life, about her youth in Germany and coming of age in Palestine, about her loves, her paintings, and how the Resistance had punished her for consorting with a British officer, Ann's father. Then she told what I already knew about Edith's affairs with Heinrich Rosenthal and Rudy Schwartz and the two pictures she had drawn before leaving for England. 'Those two pictures are your mother,' Edith wrote to the daughter she hardly knew. She begged Ann to find them. 'They are my most precious works. Heinrich and Rudy don't need them anymore. They will forget me. But you must know my face.'

Ann gave me a questioning look. 'They didn't forget her,' I answered quickly. 'She wasn't easy to forget. But go on with the story.'

Her mother's letter and her beloved father's death brought about a change in her life. She began to feel a strong connection with Judaism and with Israel, and she started reading books about Jewish history and attending a synagogue in London; she had a meeting with an 'aliyah' representative, and from there it was a short step to settling in Israel. She even began using her mother's maiden name – Strauss.

I sat there listening, thinking about the strangeness of fate. Mr Rosenthal had emigrated from Germany. So had Edith, who wound up in England only to have her daughter return here so many years later. Ann continued her story. She had been in Israel for a year and a half, at Kibbutz Kiryat Anavim outside Jerusalem. She was constantly tormented by the thought that she hadn't fulfilled her mother's last request, so she decided to visit Rudy Schwartz. Rudy was suspicious, and before she could open her mouth, he accused her of spying on him, 'Or maybe you're here to collect money for some dubious charity.' But suddenly she saw it, behind him on the shelf, the picture of the living, laughing mouth – the mouth of her mother.

'So you went ahead and stole it,' I said

angrily. It was incredible though – she seemed too nice to do a thing like that.

'You don't understand,' she said. 'It was a memento from my mother, and he was such an awful man, I didn't steal it –'

'What?' I jumped up. If Ann wasn't the thief, the danger had not yet passed.

'What I mean is, I did take it,' she explained awkwardly. 'That is, I borrowed the picture – I took it from Mr Schwartz, but a little while later it was on its way back to him. Don't you understand?'

No, I didn't understand.

'Now look here!' she said, red with anger, 'I am not a thief! The picture was very precious to me, yes – but I couldn't keep it knowing it was stolen. I preferred to leave it with that awful man than to steal it. You see, I . . . Now do you understand?' She was almost pleading. I nodded.

'But what did you do with the picture?' I asked.

She laughed bitterly. 'I took it out of the frame and photocopied it. All I have is a pale copy. I put Schwartz's picture back in the frame and mailed it off to him. He's probably received it by now.

I gazed at her in wonder. She had no idea of the mess she'd made. 'And that . . . that arrangement,' I asked tactfully, trying not to hurt her feelings, 'was that what you were planning to do with Mr Rosenthal's picture?'

'Yes,' she answered meekly, avoiding my eyes. 'Look, I know what you must think of me, but I didn't realise anyone would be hurt by it. Rudy Schwartz probably never even noticed that the picture was missing for a minute or two. And I'm sure your grandfather wouldn't have noticed either.'

'Mr Rosenthal? He isn't my grandfather,' I said. 'he's my friend.' Then I glanced at my watch. It was two thirty. 'Ann, listen,' I said as calmly as I could. 'You don't know what you've done. Two men might be killed in a duel on account of your recklessness. But I don't want to waste time now, so let me just say this: if you agree to do what I

tell you, it may turn out all right for everyone.' I spoke clearly and distinctly, and I
think my father – who's a lawyer – would
have been proud of me. 'And another thing'
I said, 'if you do what I tell you, you might
get the original pictures from Rudy
Schwartz and Heinrich Rosenthal, and you
won't have to be satisfied with a copy.' I
saw the look of doubt in her eyes. I knew
our chances were slim, but I had this crazy
idea. 'Vera's antique shop will be open
soon,' I said, 'on our way over, I'll fill you
in about Vera. Let me just have a moment
to think in quiet first.' She looked at me in
wide-eyed surprise. I may have sounded a
little conceited, but I had to make her trust
me so she'd agree to the plan.

'And what am I supposed to do while
you're thinking?' she asked with some
amusement, reminding me that I was only
twelve years old after all.

And then I had a really brilliant idea. I
explained to her. She hesitated at first, but
then I told her that if she agreed to it, I'd

forgive her for the scare she'd given me. She laughed. She agreed. We found some paper and a pen, and spent the next few minutes, with me as Sherlock Holmes on Mr Rosenthal's bed, planning out our next moves, and with Ann Strauss at his desk, writing out a five page composition in simple English entitled 'A Day in the Life of George, the Boy from London'.

## CHAPTER ELEVEN

# The Duel

Vera arrived at her shop on Hertzl Boulevard at exactly three o'clock, one hour before the duel in the apple orchard, and remember, Mr Rosenthal's gun wasn't loaded. There were three things I was counting on: Vera's car, her shop, and her quick thinking. I tested these in reverse order. She breezed through the quick thinking test. I introduced her to Ann. 'She's the daughter of Edith Strauss, the artist we were talking about earlier.' Vera shook her hand. '*Gottsolhelfen!*' she said. 'She's the image of her mother!' But there was no time for explanations. 'Vera,' I said, 'something terrible is going to happen and we have to get to the apple orchard near Kibbutz Ramat Rachel right away. Otherwise

Heinrich Rosenthal will be killed, do you understand?'

She didn't understand. I'd been talking to everyone in riddles for the past few hours, making strange proposals and preposterous plans. God only know how I got myself into such a fix – was it nerve, or childish stupidity? In any case, there was no time to waste.

Vera nodded with beaming eyes and I knew she would help. That made me feel a little better. Vera is really special, and I was glad to have her on my side. Now we had to search the shop – to hunt through Vera's merchandise, that is. I explained my plan to Vera and Ann. They were sceptical. I said it was the only way Ann would ever be able to get her mother's pictures back. They still look unconvinced. I said it was also the only way we could prevent the duel. That convinced them.

We dived into the piles of junk in the storeroom, pitching Vera's wares in the air and raising ancient shafts of dust. Now and again Vera would grab something off a hidden shelf, or use a hook to pull down a hanger from the ceiling, and then we would gather around for a look at the goods. I strained my eyes in the dark, and my memory too, trying to match things up, then tossing them aside – no, that wouldn't do – it had to be absolutely perfect, an exact replica. Ann joined in the search. It was fun to watch her wading through the clothes and the boxes, crawling around the suitcases and the antique sewing kit, banging her head against the wooden lamps, without a word of complaint.

And then at three thirty when we were all getting pretty discouraged and I was ready to scratch the plan and leave for the apple orchard, Vera found what we'd been looking for. It must have been waiting for us there in the storeroom for a good thirty years. I went outside, and four minutes later, Ann and Vera emerged, with beaming smiles on their faces. I clapped my hands. That was just how I'd imagined her! But we had to get a move on, it was twenty minutes to four, and time was running out.

We jumped into Vera's jalopy, and Ann took a mirror out of her purse and fixed her hair according to instructions. Then she turned around to me in the back seat, made a face, and gave me a wink and a smile. She looked absolutely terrific, and I was sure my plan would work.

The car groaned with pain every time Vera stepped on the gas. She tore past the other cars, her nose pressed closed to the windshield. Meanwhile I gave her and Ann a full account of everything that had happened, starting the day before, when Mr Rosenthal received the threatening letter, and working backwards through rings of time, to his student days in Heidelberg, from there to Jerusalem in the thirties and forties, then to England, where Edith died and Ann was born, and back to Jerusalem in the sixties.

I couldn't see Ann's face from where I sat, but I could see the back of her neck – and the back of her neck said a lot. It said that she was worried, and then it seemed to wince with remorse. We rode along in silence.

We got there at five minutes to four and parked near the apple orchard. I jumped out of the car. I had already told Ann exactly what to do – and when. The 'when' was very important and I hoped she'd understood me and that we weren't too late.

It started to drizzle and I ran out as fast as I could. I knew exactly where to go because I could see a small crowd standing in the middle of the orchard. This was a difficult moment for me: I was afraid I'd failed, that my childish urge to have a big dramatic scene had made me late for the duel. I felt a cold, clammy fear in my fluttering heart and heard Mom's voice saying, 'You live in a make-believe world David, and sometimes you just don't seem to know the difference between reality and fantasy.' How right she was. I was afraid I'd fatally confused the two this time, and I hated myself for looking at life and the people around me as if they were part of some imaginary story I was writing.

The crowd turned in surprise as I ran up. We stood there staring at each other.

They all wore long dark overcoats and carried black umbrellas. They were bent with age, and their faces were creased and wrinkled. At first they appeared to me like some strange painting, and then their faces started to look familiar. I knew them! They were Mr Rosenthal's cronies from Café Stern, his Senior Citizens' Patrol. A little way off I could see Mr Rosenthal with his back to us, staring out into the distance of an Arab village, wrapped in fog. I turned to the left – and there for the first time I saw Rudy Schwartz, the bully of Heidelberg University. Had I been any less nervous than I was, and had the silence in the apple orchard been any less forbidding, I would probably have burst out laughing. For the past two days Mr Rosenthal had been telling me about the terrifying bully of

Heidelberg, and I forgot that it was fifty years since Rudy Schwartz had been such a tough guy. Oh sure, maybe he still wore a size 17 shoe, but he was hardly terrifying: he looked kind of pathetic, actually like a skinny beanpole that could snap in the breeze. But then when I saw his eyes I changed my mind. They blazed. I don't know how else to describe the fire burning in them, a fire of rage, of madness.

A little man in the crowd recognised me now and stepped forward. It was Jake Stern, the owner of the café. 'We tried to talk them out of it, friend David,' he said, his voice quivering with age. 'We tried to convince them not to go through with it, we told them it isn't worth it, not at their age, but Rudy Schwartz is adamant. We did our best, we really did.' And he smiled grimly and stepped back. Another old man, one I didn't know, grumbled, 'A code of honour, he calls it. Honour or death. You can't reason with the likes of Rudy Schwartz. The man's a savage,' and then he added something in Yiddish I didn't understand.

The other old men nodded in agreement. It started raining harder. The dark coats, the grey fog, the wind buffeting the trees – everything looked so strange I wished that Mom were there to see how the boundary line between reality and fantasy can sometimes get blurred.

But just then Rudy Schwartz cried out and the old men veered around to his direction. I crowded in line with them and turned to look. Heinrich Rosenthal and Rudy Schwartz were standing back to back. Schwartz was about twice as tall as Mr Rosenthal. They started pacing in opposite directions. Schwartz's steps were brisk, deliberate. Mr Rosenthal's were heavy and slow. It was then, for the first time since I'd know him, that I noticed Mr Rosenthal was old. His seventy years weighed heavily on his back and shoulders. His sneakers glistened in the rain.

Suddenly I realised that I had only a few seconds left to stop this farce, and I couldn't stand here dreaming! I pushed my way through the crowd and ran out to Mr Rosenthal. Heedless of the terrible danger I had placed myself in, I stood between the two of them, directly in their line of fire. I closed my eyes and screamed with all my might: 'Stop! Don't shoot, Schwartz! I've found the thief!'

And I wasn't sure whether in answer I would hear a human voice – or an exploding gun.

## CHAPTER TWELVE

# Reality or Fantasy

There was a long, deep silence. I was as tight as a fist. I stood with my eyes screwed up against the rain. I heard a small commotion in the crowd of Mr Rosenthal's friends.

'Who is this boy?' I heard the gravelly voice of Rudy Schwartz enquire. What a relief: he hadn't fired. I opened my eyes. Schwartz was standing beside me, skinny and tall, his eyes smouldering with rage – but the gun in his hands pointed down. I couldn't look at Mr Rosenthal. I had to concentrate on the ferocious Schwartz.

'Look here, Schwartz!' I said rudely. I was angry with the man and I hated him. He really was a savage, willing to kill over a mere suspicion or a distant memory. 'I know who stole your picture. You'll get it back too. It's probably at your house now.'

Schwartz gaped at me in amazement. He hadn't expected to be spoken to like this.

'Where have you come from?' he demanded. 'Who are you anyway?'

Now the old men gathered round us, and Mr Rosenthal came over and stood next to me. He looked terribly distressed, and I hated Schwartz worse than ever. 'I hope you know what you're talking about, friend David,' said Mr Rosenthal. 'I don't think I could face it a second time.'

And I knew as I stood there that I couldn't possibly talk Schwartz out of the duel. He was blind with rage, and I was afraid he would end up shooting me. I prayed that Ann had gotten the instructions right, because she was my only way out of this predicament.

'Go away, boy!' ordered Schwartz. 'Go home! Let us pick up where we left off, Rosenthal,' he said, then pivoted around and raised his gun.

And at that moment, Ann Strauss popped

out between the apple trees. She wasn't dressed in her blue-jean overalls anymore; she was wearing a beautiful long gown with puffy sleeves – an old-fashioned dress we had found in Vera's storeroom. She was no longer wearing the big glasses, of course, and her golden hair flowed out under a wide-brimmed hat with a blue feather in it. Her bright red mouth smiled gaily; she was an exact replica of Edith as I had seen her that morning in the photograph in the book of modern Jewish art. And the look on their faces when the two of them saw her! They were astounded! The guns dropped from their hands and they literally flew to Ann's side. They kissed her hands with reverence, and stood there, all three, looking like a picture in an old book of fairy-tales; and only then did I breathe in the cold damp air, close my eyes, and sigh with relief.

All this happened sixteen years ago, but when I sat down to write the story, I was perfectly confident that I would remember all the important details. And how could I forget them, when every year on the 20 October, the anniversary of the duel that almost took place, all of us meet at a café to celebrate and reminisce.

By all of us I mean Mr Rosenthal, who is still a sprightly old man though he's well into his eighties; Vera, who still drives her old jalopy and runs the antique shop where no one ever browses; and Ann Strauss, today Ann Lapidot, the mother of two girls and a baby boy (her oldest daughter, incidentally, is named after Edith). Some of Mr Rosenthal's other friends turn up too, like Jake Stern, former owner of Café Stern, which doesn't exist anymore.

Is anyone curious to know what happened to Schwartz? Let me tell you. When Ann popped out between the trees in the apple orchard and explained her deed, Schwartz offered her his picture, the portrait of Edith's mouth. Ann said she knew how important the picture was to him and she didn't want to deprive him of it, but Schwartz insisted that she keep the picture, though he hoped he could visit occasionally for a peek at it. Ann, of course, agreed.

And visit he did, first at Kibbutz Kiryat Anavim, and later in Jerusalem, where Ann moved after her marriage. Schwartz didn't join our yearly gatherings, but Ann kept in touch with him and said he was very fond of her children. When she described little Edith climbing up on Schwartz's lap, I began to suspect that there was something human about him after all, though even now I can't help bearing him a grudge.

Heinrich Rosenthal still strolls around Jerusalem in his sneakers, with the old box camera dangling from his shoulder. The years have hardly changed him, though now he walks with a shiny-tipped cane (which I found for him in the back of Vera's shop). He still lives in his room at the Beit Hakerem Home for the Aged, where he keeps the old grey suitcase with the two cloth belts. Needless to say, he too offered Ann his picture, the portrait of Edith's tender eyes, her other face. Ann tells me that often when he visits her, he holds the picture up and gazes at it. Describing his love for her mother to Ann, he explained, 'It was impossible, but as often happens, that very impossibility is what made it so alluring.'

I remembered his words when I sat down to write this story. They'll never believe me, I thought to myself. A duel in Jerusalem, in the middle of the sixties?!'

But thinking about Mr Rosenthal, I decided to write this story down, fantasy and all – and the boundaries between reality and fantasy became faded and blurred, just as they are in life.